THIS BOOK BELONGS TO

. . . .

THE TALE
OF
MRS. TIGGY-WINKLE

THE TALE OF
MRS. TIGGY-WINKLE

BY

BEATRIX POTTER

Author of
"The Tale of Peter Rabbit", &c.

FREDERICK WARNE

*The reproductions in this book have been made using
the most modern electronic scanning methods from entirely
new transparencies of Beatrix Potter's original watercolours.
They enable Beatrix Potter's skill as an artist to be appreciated
as never before, not even during her own lifetime.*

FREDERICK WARNE

Published by the Penguin Group
27 Wrights Lane, London W8 5TZ, England
Penguin Books USA Inc., 375 Hudson Street, New York, New York 10014, USA
Penguin Books Australia Ltd, Ringwood, Victoria, Australia
Penguin Books Canada Ltd, 2801 John Street, Markham, Ontario, Canada L3R 1B4
Penguin Books (NZ) Ltd, 182-190 Wairau Road, Auckland 10, New Zealand

Penguin Books Ltd, Registered Offices: Harmondsworth, Middlesex, England

First published 1905
Published with new reproductions 1987
This paperback edition first published 1991

Printed and bound in Great Britain by
William Clowes Limited, Beccles and London

for
THE REAL LITTLE LUCIE
OF NEWLANDS

ONCE upon a time there was a little girl called Lucie, who lived at a farm called Little-town. She was a good little girl—only she was always losing her pocket-handkerchiefs!

One day little Lucie came into the farm-yard crying— oh, she did cry so! "I've lost my pocket-handkin! Three handkins and a pinny! Have *you* seen them, Tabby Kitten?"

THE Kitten went on washing her white paws; so Lucie asked a speckled hen—

"Sally Henny-penny, have *you* found three pocket-handkins?"

But the speckled hen ran into a barn, clucking—

"I go barefoot, barefoot, barefoot!"

11

12

AND then Lucie asked Cock Robin sitting on a twig.

Cock Robin looked sideways at Lucie with his bright black eye, and he flew over a stile and away.

Lucie climbed upon the stile and looked up at the hill behind Little-town—a hill that goes up—up—into the clouds as though it had no top!

And a great way up the hill-side she thought she saw some white things spread upon the grass.

LUCIE scrambled up the hill as fast as her stout legs would carry her; she ran along a steep path-way—up and up—until Little-town was right away down below—she could have dropped a pebble down the chimney!

14

15

16

PRESENTLY she came to a spring, bubbling out from the hill-side.

Some one had stood a tin can upon a stone to catch the water—but the water was already running over, for the can was no bigger than an egg-cup! And where the sand upon the path was wet—there were foot-marks of a *very* small person.

Lucie ran on, and on.

THE path ended under a big rock. The grass was short and green, and there were clothes - props cut from bracken stems, with lines of plaited rushes, and a heap of tiny clothes pins—but no pocket-handkerchiefs!

But there was something else—a door! straight into the hill; and inside it some one was singing—

"Lily-white and clean, oh!
With little frills between, oh!
  Smooth and hot—red rusty spot
Never here be seen, oh!"

18

19

LUCIE, knocked — once — twice, and interrupted the song. A little frightened voice called out "Who's that?"

Lucie opened the door: and what do you think there was inside the hill?—a nice clean kitchen with a flagged floor and wooden beams—just like any other farm kitchen. Only the ceiling was so low that Lucie's head nearly touched it; and the pots and pans were small, and so was everything there.

THERE was a nice hot
singey smell; and at the
table, with an iron in her hand
stood a very stout short person
staring anxiously at Lucie.

Her print gown was tucked
up, and she was wearing a
large apron over her striped
petticoat. Her little black
nose went sniffle, sniffle, snuffle,
and her eyes went twinkle,
twinkle; and underneath her
cap—where Lucie had yellow
curls—that little person had
PRICKLES!

22

23

24

"WHO are you?" said Lucie. "Have you seen my pocket-handkins?"

The little person made a bob-curtsey—"Oh, yes, if you please'm; my name is Mrs. Tiggy-winkle; oh, yes if you please'm, I'm an excellent clear-starcher!" And she took something out of a clothes-basket, and spread it on the ironing-blanket.

"**W**HAT'S that thing?" said Lucie—"that's not my pocket-handkin?"

"Oh no, if you please'm; that's a little scarlet waist-coat belonging to Cock Robin!"

And she ironed it and folded it, and put it on one side.

THEN she took something else off a clothes-horse—

"That isn't my pinny?" said Lucie.

"Oh no, if you please'm; that's a damask table-cloth belonging to Jenny Wren; look how it's stained with currant wine! It's very bad to wash!" said Mrs. Tiggy-winkle.

MRS. TIGGY-WINKLE'S
nose went sniffle, sniffle,
snuffle, and her eyes went
twinkle, twinkle; and she
fetched another hot iron from
the fire.

"THERE'S one of my pocket-handkins!" cried Lucie—"and there's my pinny!"

Mrs. Tiggy-winkle ironed it, and goffered it, and shook out the frills.

"Oh that *is* lovely!" said Lucie.

"AND what are those long yellow things with fingers like gloves?"

"Oh, that's a pair of stockings belonging to Sally Henny-penny—look how she's worn the heels out with scratching in the yard! She'll very soon go barefoot!" said Mrs. Tiggy-winkle.

"**W**HY, there's another handkersniff — but it isn't mine; it's red?"

"Oh no, if you please'm; that one belongs to old Mrs. Rabbit; and it *did* so smell of onions! I've had to wash it separately, I can't get out the smell."

"There's another one of mine," said Lucie.

"**W**HAT are those funny little white things?"

"That's a pair of mittens belonging to Tabby Kitten; I only have to iron them; she washes them herself."

"There's my last pocket-handkin!" said Lucie.

40

"AND what are you dipping into the basin of starch?"

"They're little dicky shirt-fronts belonging to Tom Tit-mouse—most terrible particular!" said Mrs. Tiggy-winkle. "Now I've finished my ironing; I'm going to air some clothes."

"WHAT are these dear soft fluffy things?" said Lucie.

"Oh those are woolly coats belonging to the little lambs at Skelghyl."

"Will their jackets take off?" asked Lucie.

"Oh yes, if you please'm; look at the sheep-mark on the shoulder. And here's one marked for Gatesgarth, and three that come from Little-town. They're *always* marked at washing!" said Mrs. Tiggy-winkle.

43

AND she hung up all sorts and sizes of clothes—small brown coats of mice; and one velvety black mole-skin waist-coat; and a red tail-coat with no tail belonging to Squirrel Nutkin; and a very much shrunk blue jacket belonging to Peter Rabbit; and a petticoat, not marked, that had gone lost in the washing —and at last the basket was empty!

T HEN Mrs. Tiggy-winkle
made tea—a cup for her-
self and a cup for Lucie. They
sat before the fire on a bench
and looked sideways at one
another. Mrs. Tiggy-winkle's
hand, holding the tea-cup, was
very very brown, and very very
wrinkly with the soap-suds;
and all through her gown and
her cap, there were *hair-pins*
sticking wrong end out; so
that Lucie didn't like to sit
too near her.

47

48

WHEN they had finished tea, they tied up the clothes in bundles; and Lucie's pocket-handkerchiefs were folded up inside her clean pinny, and fastened with a silver safety-pin.

And then they made up the fire with turf, and came out and locked the door, and hid the key under the door-sill.

THEN away down the hill trotted Lucie and Mrs. Tiggy-winkle with the bundles of clothes!

All the way down the path little animals came out of the fern to meet them; the very first that they met were Peter Rabbit and Benjamin Bunny!

51

A^{ND} she gave them their nice clean clothes; and all the little animals and birds were so very much obliged to dear Mrs. Tiggy-winkle.

SO that at the bottom of the
hill when they came to
the stile, there was nothing
left to carry except Lucie's
one little bundle.

LUCIE scrambled up the stile with the bundle in her hand; and then she turned to say "Good-night," and to thank the washer-woman— But what a *very* odd thing! Mrs. Tiggy-winkle had not waited either for thanks or for the washing bill!

She was running running running up the hill — and where was her white frilled cap? and her shawl? and her gown—and her petticoat?

57

58

A ND *how* small she had
grown—and *how* brown
—and covered with PRICKLES!
Why! Mrs. Tiggy-winkle
was nothing but a HEDGEHOG.

★　　★　　★　　★

(Now some people say that little
Lucie had been asleep upon the stile—
but then how could she have found
three clean pocket-handkins and a pinny,
pinned with a silver safety-pin?

And besides—*I* have seen that door
into the back of the hill called Cat
Bells—and besides *I* am very well
acquainted with dear Mrs. Tiggy-winkle!)

Some other Beatrix Potter books

The Complete Tales of Beatrix Potter

The Miniature World of Peter Rabbit:
12–Copy Box

Beatrix Potter's Countryside Book

The World of Peter Rabbit Sticker Book

The World of Peter Rabbit Postcard Book

My Photograph Album: a
Beatrix Potter Keepsake

Beatrix Potter Posters